Stella Tells Her Story

by Janiel Wagstaff
Illustrated by Dana Regan

For Max:
May you fearlessly write your own life narrative.
I believe in you and love you way past the moon and back!

No part of this book may be reproduced in whole or in part, or stored in a retrieval system, or transmitted in any form or by any means, electronic, mechanical, photocopying, recording, or otherwise, without written permission of the publisher. For information regarding permission, write to Scholastic Inc., 557 Broadway, New York, NY 10012.

ISBN: 978-1-338-26475-3
Copyright © 2018 by Janiel Wagstaff
Illustrations: Dana Regan © Staff Development for Educators
All rights reserved. Printed in Jiaxing, China.

2 3 4 5 6 7 8 9 10   68   23 22 21 20 19 18

"A puppy! A puppy! We got a puppy yesterday!" Max is so struck by puppy love, he's shouting it to everyone at the coat rack.

Lots of kids gathered round to hear him, including me.

I'm Stella.

"She has the softest fur and licks my face so much it tickles," Max added.

Our second grade class is mesmerized.

Everyone asked Max questions. We were so busy, Ms. Merkley had to come out of the classroom to bring us in to start the day. She wasn't mad. In fact, instead of doing our morning math, she called us over to the rug. She said today was the perfect day to start writing narratives.

Narrative seems like a big word, but it just means stories. We all have stories to tell! Sometimes story ideas are big and exciting and other times they're just small. But every day there are events or happenings in our lives we can write about.

Ms. M (as we call her) wrote the word TOPICS in big red letters on one side of the whiteboard and said this would be our special place to record ideas that we could turn into stories. Ideas are all around us, just waiting to be noticed! "Max's Puppy" was the first topic to go on our list.

"I know, I know! I have a story, too!" Ms. M called on Tineka.

"I went up to the lake with my uncle, and we caught this really ugly fish. I freaked out because it was squirmy and wet, and its gills were flapping."

"What did it look like?" Simon asked.

"It was big and gray and green and brownish! And, it had these pointy things coming out from its mouth. It looked right at me, and I screamed!"

Kids started getting excited, talking about whatever was bouncing around in their heads. Ms. M had to stop us.

"Okay, class, I see you're fired up. Don't worry, we want to hear everyone's story. But, let's take a minute and come back to Tineka's. It sounds like you caught a catfish."

"Yeah, yeah, that's what my uncle called it."

"What did you do with it?"
This time it was Charlie.
He got all googley-eyed,
like he'd never seen a fish before.
I guess that's what hearing good stories can do to you.

"We took the hook out and threw it back in the lake.
I was so glad. I didn't want to be on the boat with that thing staring at me!"

Ms. M went back to the board. Under TOPICS, she added "Tineka's Catfish." She could tell we all wanted a chance to talk, so she let us turn to our neighbors and share our story ideas. Kids who couldn't think of anything yet just listened in; maybe hearing our ideas would help them get started.

I told Kyle about making chocolate cupcakes over the weekend with my mom. I ended up with batter on my face and all stringy through my hair! My idea must have helped him think of his own because he told me about making big fat mud pies in the park. I guess he got in trouble when he got home. Moms don't like head-to-toe mud splotches!

Ms. M walked around listening to our conversations, and then, under TOPICS, she wrote a couple of the ideas she heard.

"Many of you seem ready to write. Talking about our stories really helps. Here are some other tricks writers use."

She grabbed a big sheet of paper and wrote FIRST, NEXT, THEN, and LAST down the side. "Stories need a beginning, middle, and end. Writers sometimes start by thinking of a happening or event or even a moment from their lives. They think, *What happened at the beginning? What happened next?*, and so on."

"Let's try it with Max's story. Max, you got a puppy yesterday, right?"

"Yep."

"What happened first?"

"I went with my mom and brother to the animal shelter to look at puppies."

"Tell us a little more about that. How did you pick *your* dog?"

"We picked her because she really liked us! She was wagging her tail, whining, and jumping all over the place. It looked like she was smiling at us!"

"Those are great details for your story! What happened next?" While Ms. M asked Max for details, she wrote on the big paper.

"See class, I'm jotting notes to help us remember the important things that happened FIRST, NEXT, THEN, and LAST in Max's story. Good writers do this all the time to figure out what they're thinking, organize their thoughts, and plan their stories. If they have trouble, they can ask a friend to listen and ask questions, just like you saw me doing. Soooooo... who's ready to write?"

A sea of hands shot up. I couldn't wait to get hold of some paper!

Okay, first, my happening—my event. What should I tell about? Cupcake hair? I heard one of the other kids talking about his grandma and that made me think of a time last year with my Oma. Hmmmm... that was a good event.

Okay, organizing. What happened? In order. I think I'll try that jotting thing with those special words to help me.

First Mom promissed my first roller coster ride at super fun land!!, Oma is coming with us.

next We get crazy! Mom yells!! at us!! So we slow down.

then Milo gets sick and goes with Mom
I wait with Oma
All of a sudden SHE wants to go on the roller coster !
I am scared!
Oma says she'll hold my hand the whole time
We GO!

Last sqeezed hands so tight
It was scary !! but fun
Big smiles! ☺
We go to find Milo and Mom

That was some fantastic advice Ms. M gave. She's a great writer. Those FIRST, NEXT, THEN, LAST words and that jotting really got me going. My story's all planned!

Now I'll write it down all story-ish. Ms. M says to pretend you're telling the story to your partner again, only this time, use the list to help you. Okay, here goes.

**Off we went to Super Fun Land!
Milo and I were so excited.**

Today was extra special. Mom promised to take me on my first-ever roller coaster ride! Plus, we were going with Oma.

Mom told us Oma was coming just to walk and enjoy time with us. She wouldn't be able to go on any rides, and we had to walk slowly. We said okay. But, when we finally got inside the park, Milo and I went a little craaaazy.

We saw all those rides and games and popcorn and candy.

"I want to go here. I want to go there! I want cotton candy! I want soda pop!" we yelled. Mom got mad and yelled at *us!*

Mom doesn't yell very often, so Milo and I put a lid on it. I held Oma's hand on one side and Milo held her hand on the other.

We walked really s l o w l y.

After a few rides, sodas, and giant rainbow lollipops, Milo started looking a bit sick and complaining his stomach hurt.

Mom said he just needed a rest and took him to sit in the shade. Off they went . . . right when we were coming up to the roller coaster! Oma and I just stood there.

Suddenly Oma said, "Let's go. I'll ride it with you."

I was sure Mom and Milo would be gone a while, but that one threw me for a loop. I said, "Oh no, I'm really scared!"

Oma told me not to worry. She said she would hold my hand the whole way.

"Really, the whole way?" I wasn't so sure about this, I mean, how old is Oma anyway?

"Yes, honey, the whole way. Let's go."

Oma grabbed my hand and we got in line. I think I started shaking, but Oma smiled and held on tight.

When we got to the coaster, one of the workers helped me and Oma get in. We put on the belt and waited. I squeezed her hand even tighter.

Swoosh! We raced to the top of a super enormous hill and then came roaring down.

My stomach was in my mouth! I was thrown around the seat, but Oma still held on.

I didn't even dare look over at her. I think my eyes were mostly, pretty much, all the way closed.

SLAM. It was over. We flew forward, but the belt held us back. Now *my* stomach hurt!

We came down the ramp with big smiles.
Then we went to find Mom and Milo.

There. I like it. A special story about me and my Oma.

Ms. M listened in as I read my story to Kyle. He liked it 'cause he loves roller coasters. Ms. M said it reminded her of the first time she took a ride in a helicopter because that made her scared, too. She said I had a really strong beginning and middle, but I might want to consider doing more with the ending. Kyle agreed.

He asked, "What did your Oma think of the ride?" I thought that was a good question. Endings are sometimes hard, you know. Let's see, what did I have on my jotting for LAST? Hmmmm... "It was scary, but fun." Well, that doesn't sound very interesting, and it doesn't answer Kyle's question, either.

Oma had fun! She was smiling BIG.
And I was smiling BIG.

That sounds okay. But, I keep thinking about Oma grabbing my hand, leading me up to the ride, and holding tight the whole time like she promised. Let me try something with that.

Oma was still holding my hand as we came down the ramp. When she let go, it was all red and squished, and it kind of hurt. But, we did it! We rode the roller coaster!

Ms. M always tells us to go back and reread our work. I did. This second ending is way, way better. It makes me feel proud. I love it!

Me, Oma and The Roller Coster

Off we went to Super Fun Land! Milo and I were so excited! Mom promissed to take me on my first ever rotter coster ride. Oma was coming to. We had to be extra well behaved because Oma is so old. But when we got inside the park, we went a little craaaazy!! We saw all those rides and games and popcorn and candy. I ran one way. Milo ran anothr way. Mom got mad and yelled at us! So we walked really S l o w, holding onto Oma.

After rides, sodas, and giant rainbow lolipops Milo complaned his stummck hurt. Mom took him to rest in

TWO WEEKS LATER

You remember how I told you the roller-coaster story happened a year ago? Well, since then my Oma got sick and has been living in a nursing home. She seems to have forgotten a lot of stuff.

We were getting ready for a visit and I thought, "I'll take my story and read it to Oma!" Ms. M and Mom thought that was a super-duper idea. Ms. M even made a copy I could leave with Oma. I wrapped it up with a bow.

So, here's what happened. Oma was kind of slouched over as usual, just sitting there in her chair. I ran up and told her I had the greatest, most special thing to share. I sat down next to her and read my story.

Guess what? She remembered!

She smiled and said, "I remember that, Stella. Your first coaster ride." And then she took my hand and held it for a very, very long time.

Welcome to Stella's world!
I'm thrilled to share Stella's adventures in writing with you.

I've been teaching elementary school for almost 30 years and have loved writing with students from day one. It's just delightful to watch them grow and discover their unique voices on paper. My first goal is always to get students to LOVE writing. But I find that engaging, concrete models of students who love to write are in short supply.

That's how Stella came to life. She's a feisty, intelligent second grader who takes on writing tasks with confidence, employs many useful strategies, and perseveres through the tough parts to get to the writing joy. She's fun. And her stories of writing are fun. Even with increased rigor and higher standards, writing should be fun and purposeful for children. Always. You'll find this to be true across all four of the Stella Writes books. Stella is a powerful mentor and will be a true inspiration for your students.

Stella Tells Her Story opens with Max, one of Stella's classmates, ecstatically telling his friends about his new puppy. Just as their teacher, Ms. Merkley (or Ms. M, as her students fondly call her), takes full advantage of the excitement generated by his oral storytelling, you should invite students to share their stories aloud with one another in informal ways. Listen closely and ask students questions to extend their thinking. Let them know by your genuine response that their stories are valuable and interesting. Students will get ideas as they listen to others' stories and come to see, as Stella says, "We all have stories to tell."

Start listing some of your students' ideas on a class Topics List (as you see on page 6). Add to the list over time to model how story ideas can pop up anytime, anywhere. When you're ready to have students begin writing their stories on paper, pick a topic and author from the list (just as Ms. M picked Max on page 12) and ask the student questions: *What happened at the beginning?* Query for more details: *What happened next?* Ask more probing questions: *Then what?* Again, query for details: *And, last?* As you engage a student in front of the class, jot down keywords from his story using transition words, such as *First, Next, Then,* and *Last* (page 13). By now, just as in the book, most students will be chomping at the bit to start writing their own stories. Ask the class: *Who's ready to write?* Direct those students who are ready to organize their ideas by jotting key words, just as you have modeled. (Stella does this on page 15—a perfect example to show your class.) If some students still feel apprehensive, gather them together to continue supporting their oral storytelling. Ask questions. Encourage. Soon, even those who are reluctant will be ready to give it a try. If not, allow them to circulate the room, noticing what other writers are doing for inspiration.

Once students have their ideas planned or even sketched out a bit, have them narrate their stories to partners, using their pre-writes as guides. You can model this with a student in front of the class first, inviting her to tell her story, talking it out in full sentences to "sound like a story." When children do this they often add details, so be sure to have the student add those to her notes as the class observes. Naturally, you can also ask questions. Afterwards, have a class discussion about what you did (listened actively and asked questions) and what the author did (told the story in full sentences, added details, wrote these in notes). Then send students off with partners to do the same. The more children tell their stories aloud, the more details they will generate, and the more successful they will be writing their stories on paper. Oral language is the ultimate scaffold to writing! (Hear Stella talk out and record her story from her notes beginning on page 16.)

Note how Ms. M listens in as Stella shares her story with Kyle (page 22). She shows real interest, makes a connection from Stella's story to a time in her life—thus, truly valuing the work—then pushes the writer to consider a revision. Stella's partner, Kyle, asks a good question, which Stella takes seriously as she reconsiders her ending. Share this beautiful scenario with students to demonstrate how they can support one another in your writing community.

As she continues with the writing process, Stella tries a few different endings for her story, going back to her notes to spark her thinking, recording some of her ideas, then rereading them out loud until she comes up with something that works (pages 23–25). Point out these useful strategies to your students and invite them to try some out when working on revisions. Be sure to show students Stella's draft (page 26), noting the changes she's made using carats, cross-outs, even correcting conventions (she changed the lowercase *w* to a capital *W* to start the fifth sentence). Likewise, celebrate these proofs of revision in your own students' drafts by putting them under the document camera or taking pictures of their work and projecting them. Celebrate, celebrate, celebrate the active work, the ideas, the application of strategies, the taking of risks! As you share their work, encourage your authors to comment on the revisions they made and why they made them.

Our story doesn't end with the "finished" product, which, as you may have noticed, is simply a draft. Stella decides to share her narrative as a gift for her Oma (page 27). When students have an authentic audience, their motivation to write skyrockets. They learn writing has real purpose. This is a core idea throughout the Stella Writes series that I cannot emphasize enough. As teachers, we need to always consider how students might share their work with an outside audience. It may not always be possible, but it often is, especially in the Internet age.* When we show children the power of their writing we have indeed given them an amazing gift.

Stella Tells Her Story is just one book in a series of four. *Stella Writes an Opinion, Stella and Class: Information Experts*, and *Stella: Poet Extraordinaire* cover opinion, informative, and poetry writing, respectively. Writers should have a balanced experience, and Stella is standing by, ready to assist students joyfully as they explore other forms of and purposes for writing!

Additional information for using the books in your instruction is available online at **www.scholastic.com/ stellawrites.** You'll find error-free copies of the texts Stella writes, her pre-writes and drafts, classroom-tested strategies to help students write across genres, and suggestions for using the books with varied grade levels.

I love teaching with picture books, just like students love listening to and learning from them. It's a dream come true to bring a character like Stella into students' writing lives through this medium. I know your students will love writing alongside her! Enjoy!

—Janiel Wagstaff

*Please note: We can't possibly have a real-world purpose for all the writing students do, nor should we. It's critical to write with students daily across the curriculum, as well as involve them in the types of writing covered in the Stella Writes titles. Most of the writing they do should be informal, with only a few projects going through the additional work needed for publication. This notion is explored in depth in the online materials that accompany the Stella series.

Stella Writes Set

TEACHING GUIDE

by Janiel Wagstaff

Hello, and welcome to the Stella Writes series! You have in your hands four books that came to life as a result of my 30 years of experience teaching young writers. Each book contains real scenarios that have occurred in my classrooms, and Stella is a composite of the writers I've worked with. She's confident, persistent, goal oriented, willing to take risks, and meant to inspire your writers as a joyful peer model they can relate to and love. I've seen over and over again, from kindergarten to fourth-grade classrooms, how Stella's personality and down-to-earth hard work ignites interest, motivates students to write across genres, and empowers them as people who have stories to tell, opinions and information to share, and poetry to explore. When you use these books, students will know their voices matter, just like Stella's and her classmates' voices do! I hope you're ready to listen and celebrate!

Here are a few general strategies for using the series as a teaching tool. Be sure to refer to the last pages of each book (pages 31 and 32) for specific ideas for each title.

Reading the Stella Books

The Stella books are meant to be read in parts—not as single read-alouds, although that is an option. Each book begins by introducing the genre students will write in, followed by explicit steps and strategies for teaching the particular text type. The text breaks into logical chunks, so it's easy to find places to stop and explore steps or strategies with your students. For example, in *Stella Tells Her Story*, Ms. Merkley (or Ms. M, as her students fondly call her) begins by explaining what a narrative is, then honors Max and Tineka by letting them tell parts of their stories to the group, and finally invites students to tell some of their own stories to one another. When reading this section to your class, find a logical stopping point and allow students to share their story ideas aloud. Then, you can read a bit more and continue, recording some of your students' topic ideas on the board, just as Ms. M does. That may be enough for the day. On the following day, you can pick up where you left off.

Teachers often spend a week and a half to two weeks working through one Stella book, since they write with students along the way. Naturally, the instructional techniques shown in each book are not the only ways to teach a genre. However, I've included a variety of practices across the four books in hopes of stretching your teaching repertoire.

If you are a kindergarten or first-grade teacher, you might read the books to your class in an abbreviated fashion if there seems to be too much covered. Read the books to yourself beforehand to note sections that will be particularly useful for the needs of the majority of your students. Mark these portions with sticky notes to guide your reading and teaching. You can always go deeper using additional portions of the texts with small groups.

As mentioned earlier, enjoying the Stella books as read-alouds is another option. Teachers who have already done a unit of study on a particular genre often use the Stella books as yet another way to breathe new life into that genre, to generate excitement and purpose for writing, or to find connections between the work their students have done and the plethora of strategies found in the books.

Writing With Stella

After you've worked through each title once, you can then repeatedly refer to the Stella books throughout your year of writing. Stella and her classmates engage in a variety of general writing strategies that you can visit and revisit with your class, sparking discussion, guided practice, and inclusion on class anchor charts. For example, in *Stella Writes an Opinion*, Stella gets stuck on her closing. Instead of giving up, she writes a couple of different endings, then leaves the writing for a while, thinking about her conclusion on the bus and at home. In the morning, she wakes to discover she has the perfect idea! Based on Stella's experience, you can add two strategies to a class anchor chart called "When Writers Get Stuck . . .":

- We attempt the hard part two or three times in different ways.
- We take a break from the writing while keeping the hard part in the back of our mind.

Revisit teaching points with the whole class, in small groups, or even with individuals. Say, for instance, you'd like to encourage a group of students to branch out individually or in pairs to write on a topic following their own interests. Review the questioning, organizing, researching, and note-taking sections of *Stella and Class: Information Experts* to stimulate discussion of this process and guide the group along their writing path. Possibilities for revisiting teaching points like these abound across the series.

Taking Time to Talk

I have to mention the role "talk" plays in the Stella books. Throughout each title, you will notice students constantly talk things through as a class, with partners, or to themselves. These talks help them develop their ideas, augment their understandings, or check and recheck the quality of their writing. One of my favorite quotes about writing comes from researcher James Britton: "Writing floats on a sea of talk." Talk is the ultimate scaffold to writing; the more we allow students to practice and develop ideas through talk, the more prepared they are to write, which increases their confidence and success.

Likewise, the more we encourage students to share their writing with one another—wherever they are in the process—the more they develop and learn the usefulness of feedback. There are many, many examples in the books. For instance, I love how a simple question posed by a classmate stirs Stella to think more deeply about her ending in *Stella Tells Her Story*. The question leads Stella in a different direction and prompts her to come up with language that captures how special the event with Oma was. This is a truly magical moment, and her revised ending captures it quite artfully. All of this happens because Ms. M recognizes the critical role talk plays in the work. Note the varied opportunities for talk throughout the books so you can incorporate more of it into your teaching. You'll see the difference in your students' attitudes and writing outcomes!

Supporting Struggling Writers

What about students who find writing difficult—those who stare at the page blankly; those who wrestle with spelling; those who are crippled by perfection; those who feel they have nothing of worth to say; or those who begin a new school year with long, sharpened pencils, fresh notebooks, and a profound dislike for writing? I thought a lot about them as I created Stella, because it's students like Stella who help lift the writing bar. Stella is a model of writing hope. And her classroom is a place of writing joy, as all classrooms should be. Stella struggles, her classmates struggle, and they are there for one another to listen and suggest, often working together on the writing, always taking their writing efforts seriously.

Explicitly point out these actions and models of grit, perseverance, and a growth mindset. Talk about the caring, involved writing community that is Stella's classroom. How does this come about? What do the students say and do? What does Ms. M say and do? Notice how she receives students' questions, insight, and ultimately their thoughts on the page with genuineness and curiosity. Note, too, how she communicates her high confidence in students' abilities, in what they know and can do, and in what they will learn. These are not "soft" teaching points. These are critical aspects of a successful writing classroom—one where students are comfortable and challenged no matter their present skill levels. This is a place where everyone will grow, where everyone has something we must take time to hear. After all, along with solid instruction, this is how we build writers.

Writing With Purpose

Each of the Stella books ends with a description of how the writing serves a purpose. In *Stella Writes an Opinion*, Ms. M shares Stella's piece with the principal, and a school policy change is made. Stella reads her story to her aging Oma in *Stella Tells Her Story*, prompting Oma to remember a touching event. The class publishes an informational book for the school library in *Stella and Class: Information Experts*. And, a poetry jam serves as a celebration at the end of the year in *Stella: Poet Extraordinaire*.

This is a HUGE theme I've tried to convey within the texts—that the writing we do with students should be purposeful so they understand the mightiness of their voices. My hope is you'll take that point to heart and look for ways to make classroom writing more purposeful, and thus, more engaging. Is there a particular audience with whom students might share their writing? Are there stakeholders who may be interested in the writing? Can you share the writing outside the classroom walls in some fashion, perhaps in a digital format? When we find these outlets, students not only get responses to their writing, but they see the power writing holds in the real world.

True, we can't do this with everything we write with students, but we can keep the idea foremost in our minds and in our planning. Often, students will have ideas for sharing their writing that are meaningful to them. Just ask them to share those! Remember, too, that simply reading a piece aloud can be a form of publishing—a form of celebration!

Lastly, keep in mind students need to write across the curriculum every day, because the more chances they have to write, the better. Daily writing opportunities deepen learning and give students more "miles on the page." Frequent, informal jots or quick writes—uncorrected and unpublished—are critically important, as they help students process content. Plus our students can't possibly be writing enough if we are taking the time to read, correct, or publish everything they produce! To learn more about this idea, visit the Stella website at www.scholastic.com/stellawrites and my personal website at www.janielwagstaff.com.

Enjoy your writing journey with students! Writing truly is the best part of my day. I hope Stella helps make this true for you and your class, too.

– *Janiel*

Purchase of this set entitles use by one teacher for one classroom only. No part of this publication may be reproduced in whole or in part, or stored in a retrieval system, or transmitted in any form or by any means, electronic, mechanical, photocopying, recording, or otherwise, without written permission of the publisher. For information regarding permission, write to Scholastic Inc., 557 Broadway, New York, NY 10012.

OTH8255193
Copyright © 2018 by Janiel Wagstaff
All rights reserved. Printed in Jiaxing, China.
2 3 4 5 6 7 8 9 10   68   23 22 21 20 19 18

Editor: Maria L. Chang
Creative Director: Tannaz Fassihi
Design by Michelle H. Kim
Illustrations by Dana Regan

Stella and Class:
Information Experts

by Janiel Wagstaff
Illustrated by Dana Regan

For the teachers of the writers and the writers themselves:
explore the magic of writing every single day!
YOU CAN!

No part of this book may be reproduced in whole or in part, or stored in a retrieval system, or transmitted in any form or by any means, electronic, mechanical, photocopying, recording, or otherwise, without written permission of the publisher. For information regarding permission, write to Scholastic Inc., 557 Broadway, New York, NY 10012.

ISBN: 978-1-338-26477-7
Copyright © 2018 by Janiel Wagstaff
Illustrations: Dana Regan © Staff Development for Educators
All rights reserved. Printed in Jiaxing, China.

2 3 4 5 6 7 8 9 10   68   23 22 21 20 19 18

Do you know what it's like to be inquisitive? To have your mind racing with questions? I do.

I'm Stella, grade two.

I wonder about a lot of things, like hot-air balloons. They're beautiful! But, how do those great big things fly?

And gymnastics. How can those gymnasts do so many flip-flop, flip-flop, flip-flops in a row like that? It's dizzying.

I'd like to find out how they do it. Maybe I could flip-flop, too!

And animals... my friends are whacko about animals, and they have a lot of questions about them.

In our class, a boy named Lucas is cheetah-crazy.

He reads EVERYTHING he can about them: books, magazines, web pages... sometimes I think he's gonna' grow whiskers and sprout spots!

So, how about you? You're a kid with an inquiring mind. What do you have questions about?

Several days ago, our second-grade class was reading a book about chameleons. It was a storybook, but we started asking all kinds of questions about *real* chameleons. Do they actually change color? Why do they have those big, bulgy eyes? Can their eyes really point in two different directions at the same time?

And, how fast are those sticky tongues? I mean, have *you* ever tried to catch a fly? Good luck! But it looks easy for chameleons. Those tongues must be fast as lightning!

Ms. Merkley, our teacher, wrote our questions on a big sheet of paper. She said, "Let's become chameleon experts! We'll answer our questions by reading several sources and checking facts on the internet. We'll jot notes as we learn. Then, we can do some informative writing to share what we find!"

Woohoo! We've done this kind of writing before. It's so exciting to find answers to our questions. Being an expert feels pretty good!

The next day, Ms. M (as we call her) brought in a bunch of information on our topic: chameleons. When we saw all those books, magazines, and articles, we were ready to dive in.

Ms. M reminded us we can't learn everything about everything about chameleons! Researchers have to stay focused. Our job was to look through the books to find information that answers our specific questions.

She pointed to our chart to remind us what we wondered about the day before. "If these are our questions, what facts should we be looking for?"

That was simple. We said, "Why chameleons change skin color! How their eyes work! How their tongues work!"

"Right," said Ms. M. "We need to stay glued to our questions." She drew three columns on the board. "We are looking for facts in these categories. When you find information, jot it on a sticky note and post it in the correct column on the board. This will help us keep our information organized."

We knew what to do: read like detectives to find answers.
I partnered up with Millie while Ms. M handed out the stickies.

We picked a magazine with an article on chameleons. We read the title and bold headings, like Ms. M has taught us, to see if the article had information in any of our categories. We also studied the photos, diagrams, and captions. There we were, focused like detectives!

And guess what? One photograph showed a chameleon's tongue darting out for a moth. Its caption said the tongue shoots out and captures the prey in a "split second!" "Ha!" I whispered to Millie. "Flash! Goodbye, moth!" She wrote a note and we dashed to the board to post our detail under TONGUES.

When we hunched back over our article, we found this: "A chameleon's tongue can be one and a half times the length of its body." In-cred-i-ble! Can you imagine having a tongue as long as you, plus another half of you?

Millie and I agreed this was a detail experts should know about chameleon tongues. Plus, we thought the other kids would go nuts for this fact! We posted another note under TONGUES.

Sticky notes soon cluttered the board. We read them one by one. Some were in the wrong columns. Some were repeats. (We decided this was actually good because we were confirming our information from several sources.) A few had information that went off topic, like where chameleons live and what they eat. (We set them aside.) When we were finished, we had plenty of details about why chameleons change color, and how their eyes and tongues work.

Over the next few days, during writing time, we looked at websites to make sure our information was accurate. I mean, if you're gonna' be experts, you'd better be sure of your facts. We even watched some short video clips online that showed chameleons changing colors, moving their eyes, and catching prey with their tongues. Then we knew we had our chameleon stuff down pat. Plus, it was amazing to see those chameleons in action!

Boy, were we ready to W R I T E! We tried a few different introductions, but nothing we wrote got us jazzed up. So, we decided to skip ahead since we were bursting with WOWZER chameleon facts! We started with what we learned about chameleons changing colors. We read back over our sticky notes and talked about each one while Ms. M quickly wrote on chart paper. Someone would say one thing, and she'd write it down. Then we'd change our minds, and she'd cross it out. Writing is a messy process! Ms. M says this is good because it shows we are thinking, rereading, and revising like good writers do.

Here's what we settled on:

Chameleons can change the color of their skin. Most people think they do this to camouflage themselves. But that is FALSE! Chameleons are already the color of their environments. They change colors when their mood or the temperature changes. They even change colors to communicate with each other. How would you like to say, "Stay away from me!" with the color of your skin? Chameleons can!

Next we wrote about chameleon eyes. We discovered they have special eye sockets that let them move their eyes in all directions.

Each eye can move on its own, so chameleons can look forward and backward at once! They can see all around them at all times so they stay safe. Can you spot a moth behind you that will make a tasty snack? Chameleons can!

The section about chameleon tongues was pretty easy:

Chameleons have super long tongues with sticky ends. When they spy their prey, they shoot out their tongues. The tongues move quick as a flash. They catch their prey in a split second! Can you catch lunch with your tongue? Chameleons can!

Francesco was so fascinated by the fact Millie and I found, he measured how long his tongue would be if he was a chameleon and drew it on poster paper. He had to tape three pieces together to show the whole tongue!

After working on our writing for several days, we decided it was finally time to write the introduction and conclusion. We studied the beginnings and endings of informational books about animals to get some ideas. One started with a question, so we thought we'd try that.

What animal can change colors, look in two different directions at once, and catch prey with the flash of a tongue? Chameleons can!

We were in l-o-v-e!

"Chameleons can" was like a theme throughout our writing. Chameleons can, chameleons can, chameleons can! What a great intro! It led us right to our conclusion. Ms. M helped us a lot on this one. It's clever, don't you think?

Chameleons are no ordinary lizards. Color change? Check. Look ahead and behind at once? Check. Snatch a bug in a flash? Check. Chameleons can!

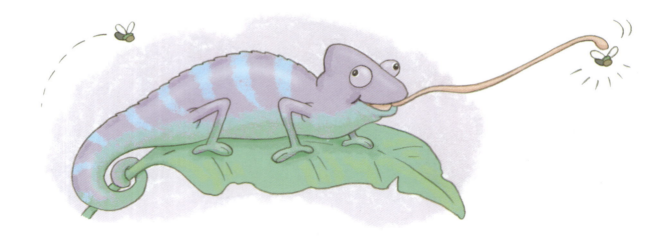

You're thinking, that was a ton of work! You're right. But it was also fun. And now we're not just chameleon experts, we're on our way to becoming informative writing experts, too. I'm ready to start investigating my own questions. Hot-air balloons and gymnastics, here I come!

TWO WEEKS LATER

Remember that storybook about chameleons? The one that got our class asking all those questions in the first place? Well, we published our own book, *Chameleons Can*, and put it in the library next to the storybook with this sign:

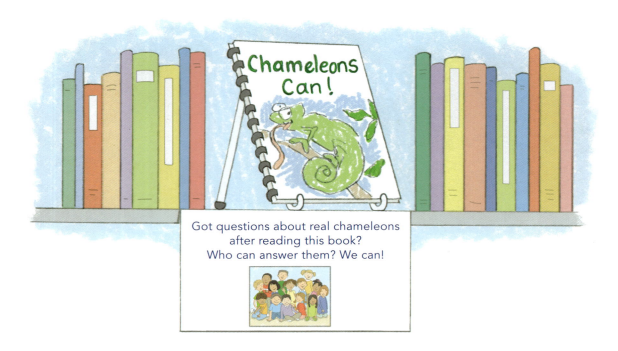

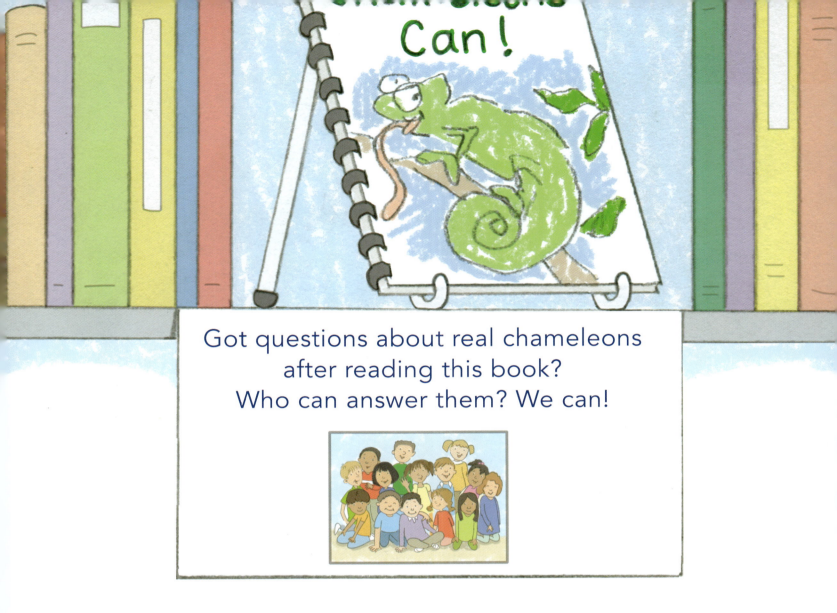

Got questions about real chameleons after reading this book?
Who can answer them? We can!

Sharing what you learn . . . that's what informative writing is all about!

Welcome to Stella's world!
I'm thrilled to share Stella's adventures in writing with you.

I've been teaching elementary school for almost 30 years and have loved writing with students from day one. It's just delightful to watch them grow and discover their unique voices on paper. My first goal is always to get students to LOVE writing. But I find that engaging, concrete models of students who love to write are in short supply.

That's how Stella came to life. She's a feisty, intelligent second grader who takes on writing tasks with confidence, employs many useful strategies, and perseveres through the tough parts to get to the writing joy. She's fun. And her stories of writing are fun. Even with increased rigor and higher standards, writing should be fun and purposeful for children. Always. You'll find this to be true across all four of the Stella Writes books. Stella is a powerful mentor and will be a true inspiration for your students.

Stella and her classmates show their inquisitive natures in *Stella and Class: Information Experts*. As their class enjoys a storybook about chameleons, students begin asking lots of questions about real chameleons (page 7). Ms. Merkley (or Ms. M, as her students fondly call her) takes full advantage of this, recognizing their curiosity as an opportunity for shared research. Cherish and celebrate this trait in your students! Encourage them to ask questions, as this can lead to shared research the way it does in Ms. M's class. When a book, video, digital presentation, or other medium inspires questions, capitalize on the moment and have students do research to find answers. Ms. M receives her students' questions with excitement, writing them down and declaring they'll become "chameleon experts" by investigating and writing about their findings (page 10). Think about how this validates students' thinking. This simple acknowledgment is critical to moving them forward into their own research as the school year progresses.

To further encourage her students, Ms. M brings in a number of chameleon sources but reminds them to stay totally focused on their questions (pages 11–12). She scaffolds this by creating a three-column chart, specifying the categories of information they'll look for as students jot on sticky notes with partners. Creating such a chart is a perfect strategy for keeping students laser-focused and to help them organize the information they find. Partners pay close attention to informative text features (e.g., bold headings, diagrams, captions) to glean important facts about their topic (page 14). Stella and Millie identify two details about chameleon's tongues that they record and add to the class chart in the proper category (pages 14–15).

Soon the chart is covered in sticky notes, and the class is ready to analyze their findings. Then they double-check their facts on websites. Again, this whole process serves as a working model for you and your class as you research a topic. Since this is shared research, you will compose using the shared writing process, as played out in detail on pages 18–26. Just like Ms. M, record students' suggestions and carefully guide them as they cooperatively negotiate what to write. Writing is a "messy process," which indicates a lot of thinking, rethinking, rechecking facts, and renegotiating sentences and paragraphs to get them just right.

Note that Ms. M's class encounters some difficulty trying to come up with an introduction (page 18). They make a few attempts, but decide to skip this portion of their writing and move right into the main ideas or chameleon fact categories. I find this to be a useful strategy when we're stuck on a section of shared writing. Let your students know that it's okay to skip a difficult part and move on, as long as they come back to it later. When Ms. M's class rereads their notes about why chameleons change skin color, they are able to write the first section of their piece (page 19). Over the course of subsequent days, they work out the sections about chameleons' eyes and tongues.

Still needing an introduction and conclusion, the class turns to mentor texts for ideas (page 25). This is a well-known and efficacious strategy. Analyzing the moves of other writers and mimicking their craft often gets the writing ball rolling and can push students over a hump or trouble spot. Ms. M's students are delighted with their solution when they try opening with a question and find the language they develop works perfectly for their conclusion, too. Such is the generative process of writing. As we compose, we discover new thoughts, new questions, and new directions. This is just what happens with Stella's class, and it can happen through the shared writing process with your class, too! Remember, the marked-up piece becomes a beautiful model to hang in the classroom so students can refer to it again and again. After all, writing is thinking, and all the changes are visible signs of that thinking and how it developed over time.

Stella reflects on the amount of effort the project took (page 27), but also on her own learning. She feels more ready than ever to tackle her own questions, bringing the book full circle to the beginning. Just as Stella takes time to reflect, allow students time to

process what they did, how they did it, and why. Discuss which parts of the writing process they might be able to take on with partners or independently as they investigate their own burning questions. (It will likely take several shared writing or other highly supportive writing experiences to get to this place.)

The story concludes with the class deciding to share their learning with a broader audience (page 28). They publish their writing in a book and position it strategically in the library next to the story that started it all.* What a purposeful way to celebrate students' efforts! Check with your librarian about making your students' writing available for reading in your library. Your students will be thrilled to think of others enjoying their words!

Stella and Class: Information Experts is just one book in a series of four. *Stella Writes an Opinion, Stella Tells Her Story*, and *Stella: Poet Extraordinaire* cover opinion, narrative, and poetry writing, respectively. Writers should have a balanced experience, and Stella is standing by, ready to assist students joyfully as they explore other forms of and purposes for writing!

Additional information for using the books in your instruction is available online at **www.scholastic.com/ stellawrites**. You'll find error-free copies of the texts Stella writes, her pre-writes and drafts, classroom-tested strategies to help students write across genres, and suggestions for using the books with varied grade levels.

I love teaching with picture books, just like students love listening to and learning from them. It's a dream come true to bring a character like Stella into students' writing lives through this medium. I know your students will love writing alongside her! Enjoy!

—Janiel Wagstaff

*Please note: We can't possibly have a real-world purpose for all the writing students do, nor should we. It's critical to write with students daily across the curriculum, as well as involve them in the types of writing covered in the Stella Writes titles. Most of the writing they do should be informal, with only a few projects going through the additional work needed for publication. This notion is explored in depth in the online materials that accompany the Stella series.

Stella Writes an Opinion

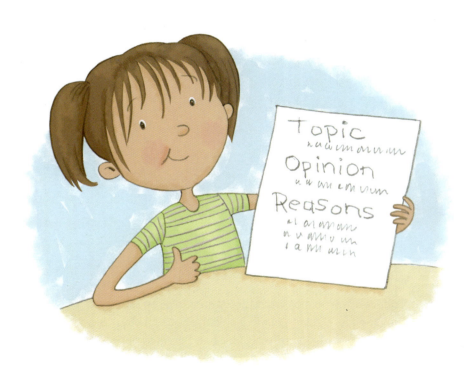

by Janiel Wagstaff
Illustrated by Dana Regan

For Lil:
In my opinion, you're the greatest niece of all! I love you!

No part of this book may be reproduced in whole or in part, or stored in a retrieval system, or transmitted in any form or by any means, electronic, mechanical, photocopying, recording, or otherwise, without written permission of the publisher. For information regarding permission, write to Scholastic Inc., 557 Broadway, New York, NY 10012.

ISBN: 978-1-338-26476-0
Copyright © 2018 by Janiel Wagstaff
Illustrations: Dana Regan © Staff Development for Educators
All rights reserved. Printed in Jiaxing, China.

2 3 4 5 6 7 8 9 10   68   23 22 21 20 19 18

Hi, I'm Stella! We do a lot of writing in our class. Today, Ms. Merkley said we get to write an opinion.

Some of the kids asked, "What's that?" I said, "Oh, that's easy. An opinion is what you think about something. It's not what your mom thinks, or your dad thinks, or your teacher or some other kid thinks; it's what *you* think."

I have so many opinions. Like, the best food is ice cream and we should be allowed to bring toys to school and Ms. Merkley is the nicest teacher in the whole world. I don't know how I'll ever choose what to write my opinion about.

Filipe and Jenny kinda' started whining. "Ms. Merkleeeeeeeee, we don't know what to write about." Can you believe that? All you have to do is think: *What do you love? What do you not-so-love? What bugs you at school or at home? What would you change if you were in charge of the world, or your class, or your bedroom?* Stuff like that.

I mean, everybody has opinions—everybody!
And what could be more fun than to write
what you think about an important topic?

Now that's power!

Remember how I said I didn't know how I'd choose what to write about? Well, I helped myself. I made a list, like good writers sometimes do. I listed all the things I love, the things I not-so-love, what bugs me about school and home, and what I'd change if I was in charge.

Then I asked myself, "Okay, which of these am I really WHOOPEE!! about?" If I was giving a speech to a sold-out crowd in my backyard, which idea would I choose? That made it easy.

See, I'm in second grade. In kindergarten and first grade we got to bring a morning snack if we wanted, you know, to keep us going 'til lunchtime. Now, we can't bring one anymore. We're too old. That bugs me, and if I was in charge, it's something I would change.

Easy.

Done.

So, this is my opinion:

Second graders should be able to bring a morning snack!

But, wait. Ms. Merkley says that isn't enough. I've only stated my topic and what I think about it. You can't just say what you want, or what bugs you, or what you'd like to change. To write a good opinion, you have to have reasons to support it.

Reasons!

Well, most of us kids are pretty good at coming up with reasons. Like when we try to get our moms to let us stay up ten more minutes at night, we can come up with about a million reasons for that. For example:

1. Reading just one more book will make us so much smarter.
2. If we stay up later, we'll be more tired and fall asleep so much faster.
3. Ten more minutes in our whole entire lifetimes doesn't really add up to much.

Stuff like that.

So, reasons. Let me think about reasons why we second graders should still be able to bring a morning snack.

Well, I hate it when my stomach grumbles right in the middle of spelling or addition. I mean, how can I concentrate on spelling words or grouping twenty-five with twenty-five with twenty when my stomach is roaring for attention?

I can't.

All I can think about is, *I'm hungry. I'm hungry. I'M HUNGRY!* So, there's a reason.

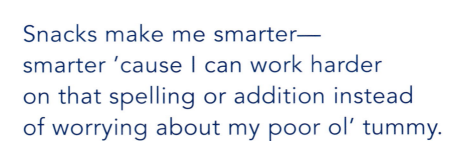

Snacks make me smarter—
smarter 'cause I can work harder
on that spelling or addition instead
of worrying about my poor ol' tummy.

Oh! I just thought of another reason!

I get grumpy when I'm hungry.

I mean grumpy like snappy at my friends or classmates.
"Don't touch that!" "I know! I know!" "Stop making that noise!"
They call this low blood sugar. Does that ever happen to you?

When you eat, you feel better, more like your usual self.

> I like to get back to my usual self
> as soon as possible, and
> a snack does the trick.

After all, most people adore the usual me.

I think those are good reasons to bring back morning snack, don't you?

So, I have my topic. I stated my opinion and my reasons for that opinion. Pretty good stuff!

Ms. Merkley says there's one more thing. Writers need to bring things to an end, like they do with stories, so we need to have a closing for our opinions. You know, like if you were giving a speech, you'd say something wise or funny that sums up your best ideas so people will remember them. This way, everyone knows you're done and can give you a standing ovation.

Hmmmm . . .
This part is not so easy. I'll try a couple of different endings on paper to see what I can do.

To sum up, snacks are needed now! Hungry stomachs turn second graders' brains to mush!

(I guess that's a little dramatic.)

How about this?

As you can see, morning snack is a good idea for growing second graders.

(That one doesn't quite sound like me.)

Sometimes I have to sit and think for a while. Sometimes I leave my writing and come back to it later.

To conclude, morning snacks are important! We should bring them back for second graders. When our stomachs are happy, we're happy kids who can learn better because we can concentrate. And, that's what school is all about.

YES!

I like that one! It sounds like me, and it reminds everyone why my opinion deserves attention. I'm glad I tried writing a few different endings, or I never would have come up with that one. I think I'm done!

But, I'll do what good writers do. I'll read it over a few times to make sure it says what I want it to say and sounds like I want it to sound.

Second graders should be able to bring a morning snack. First, we get hungry way before lunch time. If were hungry it's hard to concentrait on speling or math. It's much easyer to spell words and add numbers when our tummys are full. Snacks will help us work harder and get smarter. Second, we need snacks because some of us get low blood suger. This makes us grumpy ~~unhappy~~. We don't want to snap at our friends and snacks help us to be our usul selves. Less fighting, more sharing! Our class gets along much better that way. To conclude, morning snacks are important! We should bring them back for second graders. When our stumcks are happy, we're happy kids who can learn better because we can concentrait. And that's what school is all about.

I made a few changes. Can you find them?

Second graders should be able to bring a morning snack. ^Here's why First, we get hungry way before lunch time. If we're hungry it's hard to concentrait on spelling or math. It's much easyer to spell words and add numbers when our tummy^ies's are aren't full. grumbling so ^Snacks will help us work harder and get smarter. Second, we need snacks because some of us get low blood sugar,^a ^when we haven't eaten in awhile. This makes us grumpy unhappy. We don't want to snap at our friends and snacks help us to be our usul ^sweet selves. Less fighting, more sharing! Our class gets along much better that way. To conclude, morning snacks are important! We should bring them back for second graders. When our stumcks are happy, we're happy kids who can learn better because we can concentrait. And that's what school is all about.

TWO WEEKS LATER

Guess what?! Ms. Merkley read my opinion and thought I had some really good points. (I guess there are a few other hungry grumpy-pants people in our class besides me.) She said she wanted to show my paper to the principal, so we sat down together and fixed the misspellings. Once he read it, he agreed! We get to start bringing morning snack next week!

See, I told you opinions are powerful.

Who knows what we opinion writers might change?

Welcome to Stella's world!
I'm thrilled to share Stella's adventures in writing with you.

I've been teaching elementary school for almost 30 years and have loved writing with students from day one. It's just delightful to watch them grow and discover their unique voices on paper. My first goal is always to get students to LOVE writing. But I find that engaging, concrete models of students who love to write are in short supply.

That's how Stella came to life. She's a feisty, intelligent second grader who takes on writing tasks with confidence, employs many useful strategies, and perseveres through the tough parts to get to the writing joy. She's fun. And her stories of writing are fun. Even with increased rigor and higher standards, writing should be fun and purposeful for children. Always. You'll find this to be true across all four of the Stella Writes books. Stella is a powerful mentor and will be a true inspiration for your students.

Stella Writes an Opinion begins with Stella defining *opinion* in kid-friendly terms (see page 3) and sharing relevant examples. Be sure to pull these out for your students, emphasizing what an opinion is and perhaps generating other examples based on the models. Next, Stella offers guidance on topic selection by asking questions that are perfect for brainstorming with your class (page 5). Use these questions! Consider posting them on an anchor chart to revisit again and again as your class writes opinions throughout the year. Just as Stella generates a list of topic ideas for her opinion writing (pages 8–9), invite your students to do the same—as a class, in groups, with partners, or individually. Then allow them time to give some thought to which idea feels most important to them or as Stella says, ". . . which of these am I really WHOOPEE!! about?" This process helps students discover a topic that is important to them.

Stella goes on to write a simple opinion statement (page 11), which is a logical next step for students once they know their topics. Remind students that an opinion statement should include the topic and how they feel about it. Give them the opportunity to share these with one another, and then ask: *Once you share your opinion, what is the first question your listener wants answered?* Obviously, it is "Why? Why do you have this opinion?" Ms. Merkley announces the need for reasons and shows her class a simple graphic organizer (page 12) that you can also use to help your students organize their thinking. I love how Stella empowers writers to realize they are already good at coming up with reasons (page 13), then goes on to brainstorm two different, logical reasons to support her opinion. Her examples are useful models to study closely with your students. *Does Stella simply state a two- or three-word reason for her opinion, or does she elaborate or further explain her reason(s) with examples and feeling?* We all know generating rich reasons for opinions is challenging for our young writers. Kindergarten standards don't even require them, although I always teach them since they are so logical to include when sharing our opinions. Over time, through conversation and through writing, students will develop more skill with this element of opinion writing. Continually celebrate their attempts and ask questions to help them add details to their reasons.

Of course, even opinion writing needs a conclusion. Stella helpfully defines what a conclusion or "closing" is (page 19), then she employs several useful strategies to help her draft her final thoughts: She tries a few different endings on paper, leaves the writing and comes back to it later, then finally comes up with another ending she decides fits best (pages 21–25). Point out these processes as students work on their closings. Coming up with an effective, purposeful conclusion can actually be the most difficult part of writing. Model your own process, or mimic Stella's, thinking aloud as you do, and encourage students to simply give this their best try. Providing sentence starters like those Stella tries (e.g., "To sum up . . . ," "As you can see . . . ," "To conclude . . .") can be useful but often leads to canned endings. I sometimes ask young writers to end with a feeling. This often helps.

Lastly, Stella employs one of the best strategies we can teach our writers: rereading "to make sure it says what (we) want it to say and sounds like (we) want it to sound" (page 25). Reread, reread, reread. We can't emphasize this enough. Reread while beginning, reread in the middle, reread at the end, reread throughout. This is the only way to hear and test our voices and ideas as they develop. It is the clear path to better writing.

As the book ends, Stella's opinion writing takes on a larger purpose than a simple school assignment. Ms. Merkley helps Stella ready her piece to show the principal. Note how she simply helps fix some misspellings in her draft; she doesn't ask Stella to rewrite the whole thing! And, yes, Stella's opinion sways the principal's thinking. How empowering! I have witnessed time and time again students who, after hearing Stella's opinion and learning the power it holds,

take on a whole new perspective on opinion writing. You'll likely have students wanting to write opinions about things they'd like to change around your school. Fantastic! Make sure those opinions get to the right stakeholders (e.g., the librarian, custodian, cooks). Encourage them to write back, even if they disagree with the student. Nothing gets your students' attention faster than an outside response to their writing! It's magical to empower students by helping them find ways to share their writing beyond the classroom walls. Though we can't possibly do that with everything students write, keeping a larger, real-world purpose in mind lifts the writing we do to new heights.*

Stella Writes an Opinion is just one book in a series of four. *Stella Tells Her Story, Stella and Class: Information Experts,* and *Stella: Poet Extraordinaire* cover narrative, informative, and poetry writing, respectively. Writers should have a balanced experience, and Stella is standing by, ready to assist students joyfully as they explore other forms of and purposes for writing!

Additional information for using the books in your instruction is available online at **www.scholastic.com/ stellawrites**. You'll find error-free copies of the texts Stella writes, her pre-writes and drafts, classroom-tested strategies to help students write across genres, and suggestions for using the books with varied grade levels.

I love teaching with picture books, just like students love listening to and learning from them. It's a dream come true to bring a character like Stella into students' writing lives through this medium. I know your students will love writing alongside her! Enjoy!

—Janiel Wagstaff

---

* Please note: We can't possibly have a real-world purpose for all the writing students do, nor should we. It's critical to write with students daily across the curriculum, as well as involve them in the types of writing covered in the Stella Writes titles. Most of the writing they do should be informal, with only a few projects going through the additional work needed for publication. This notion is explored in depth in the online materials that accompany the Stella series.

Stella Writes
POETRY

Stella:
Poet Extraordinaire

by Janiel Wagstaff
Illustrated by Dana Regan

For all our young writers:
May Stella's story bring more poetry into your lives!

No part of this book may be reproduced in whole or in part, or stored in a retrieval system, or transmitted in any form or by any means, electronic, mechanical, photocopying, recording, or otherwise, without written permission of the publisher. For information regarding permission, write to Scholastic Inc., 557 Broadway, New York, NY 10012.

ISBN: 978-1-338-26478-4
Copyright © 2018 by Janiel Wagstaff
Illustrations: Dana Regan © Staff Development for Educators
All rights reserved. Printed in Jiaxing, China.

2 3 4 5 6 7 8 9 10   68   23 22 21 20 19 18

What do you think of when you hear the word *poetry*? Do you think, *Rhyme! It's time to rhyme*? Do you think, *Ugh, I hate poetry*?

Well, I'm lucky! I'm Stella, second-grade writer. I'm lucky because my teacher, Ms. Merkley (or Ms. M, as we call her), taught us from the first day of school how fun and inspiring poetry can be. Now I write at least one, maybe two, sometimes five poems a day. You can too! Ever thought of being a P-O-E-T?

Like I said, it all started on the first day of school. "It's time to go on a Poetry Walk!" Ms. M announced, smiling. "We do this every year to jump-start our writing." She took us outside with clipboards and pencils. "Poetry is all around us. Just jot down any words that come to mind for things you see, hear, or feel. You can also sketch to get your mind going. Just focus on what you're observing, and I'll show you how to turn your thinking into a poem when we return to class."

I kept staring up at the sky, so I wrote words like *sky* and *up*. I was kinda' nervous, wondering what this poetry stuff was really supposed to be about.

When we came inside, Ms. M showed us her jotting. She had written a lot more than the rest of us, but she is like 40 years old! Then she reread her words slowly; she said she was savoring them, to find the ones that stuck. "I think I'll focus my poem on the bird I observed. She sang the whole time we were outside." Ms. M tried lots of bird-words on the paper. "Hmmm, the bird was blue. I want to include that detail. And it was singing. What if I say 'sweetly singing'? I like how both those words start with the same sound."

Playground Morning Reflections
Crunch, scrunch
Crunch, scrunch
Kali walking...~~in the~~ on wood chips
~~Then~~
Chitter
Chatter
~~The bird~~ that bird-blue
Tall tree - top branch
Nonstop singing
Happy bird!
Good Morning students!
Place for Children
~~happy bright sun~~
Place to climb
Place to run
Place to scurry along the rocks (cliffs?)
Place to slide   rock-cliffs
Place to ~~swing~~ glide
~~place to~~ across the metal bars!
Place to roll/stroll
Place to join friends
Playground

She crossed out words, tried and retried, until she came up with this:

Blueish bird
on a skinny top branch
sweetly singing.
Did you have two worms
for lunch?

Gilbert worried, "I'll never be able to do that!" Ms. M said not to fret. She was sure if we played with our words like she just showed us, we'd come up with something poetic, too! "You know what, writers? Starting our year with poetry is perfect because it helps us learn to observe more closely, experiment with words freely, and discover how just a few words on the page can be powerful. Those are important things for writers to take to heart!"

So I tried with all my heart. Here's my poem from the first day:

Sky

I see sky

Staring up

So blue today

Wide

Sky

It wasn't the greatest thing I ever wrote, but it was my first poem! It was very special to me since I had captured something I would now remember from my first day of school. Plus, Ms. M says that if we read our poems slowly and "linger" (she says "linger"; I like that) on the words, they can sound pretty special. And, it's true. You've GOT to try it!

We have a board in our room called Poetry Place where we get to post our poems for others to read. Sometimes I choose to post mine, sometimes not. I write a lot of them just for myself. Ms. M says writing poetry is critical work because when you look at the world through the eyes of a poet, you might see and think of things in ways you wouldn't have before.

One time Tineka tipped her chair back. She started to fall, so she grabbed her desk. Well, the whole thing toppled over, and all her desk-stuff came flying out. Tineka felt horrible—interrupting class with the big crash! But Max suggested, "Let's write a poem about it!" So we did!

Desk Avalanche

Ms. M's talking

way too long!

I lean on back

in my chair.

Ahhhh! Feels good!

I lean way, way back.

Ahhhh! Feels bad!

I grab my desk

to catch myself.

CRASH!

It's a desk avalanche!

Crayons here,

pencils there,

books, papers everywhere!

I'm so embarrassed

I close my eyes.

Guess it's time to reorganize!

Tineka felt better, seeing the whole mess in a different way, and we all ended up cleaning out our desks! After that, we wrote lots of other quick, on-the-spot poems together.

Ms. M reads A LOT of poetry to us. A couple times a day we stop for a Poetry Break. We might be lining up to go to P.E., and she'll say, "Poetry Break!" We all stop and listen. Some of the poems are funny, rhyming stuff, good for a major laugh! Others are about everyday things, like eating lunch, catching a bug, playing with friends, or seeing lightning. I especially like those

'cause they're the ones I'm good at writing. Sometimes she reads one poem three or four times so we can really "sit with the words and feelings" (that's what she calls it). Then she asks us, "What do you think?" We share our thoughts for a few minutes, making a lot of connections to poems we could write. Usually when somebody shares a little bit, someone else gets an idea! Ideas ping-pong all over the place! We all get pretty excited, and Ms. M tells us to hurry and write down what we're thinking so it's not lost. Then, all of a sudden, we're a minute late for P.E!

Once, a poem about a dog made Sophia think about a time her dog chewed on the dining room table leg! Boy, her parents were mad! That made me think of how my cat, Cutie, pries open window blinds and stuffs her fat, furry body through the slats so she can see the birds outside.

    I wrote my idea down and came back to it later. I thought about what Cutie looks like, what she might be thinking, and I played with the words, rereading, rearranging, until I had this . . .

Fat cat

Sittin' on the table

Squeezes into the window blinds,

Halfway in and

Halfway out.

Furry thing,

She thinks the birds sound yummy!

    I'm glad I have this poem. Now, I'll always remember my silly cat and her trips through the blinds.

Another reason to write poetry is to get your feelings out. Feeling mad or sad? Write about it! You'll feel better! One day, we were supposed to go on a field trip, but there was a tornado warning. Everyone was so disappointed, but Andres was ready to explode. We went on with our math, but he got out his notebook and wrote.

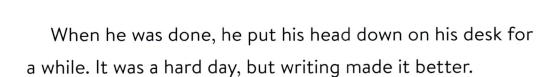

What a field trip.

We didn't even have one.

I want to RIP my papers!

I want to THROW my book.

NO field trip.

I hate tornadoes!!!!!!!

When he was done, he put his head down on his desk for a while. It was a hard day, but writing made it better.

Did you know you can write poems about things you're studying? When we studied the seasons, animal habitats, and magnets, we summed up our learning by writing class poems. Ms. M says this is a great way for us to review what we've learned, decide what is most important, and create something lasting we can come back to again and again.

This one's kinda' fun to read. Try reading the examples in parentheses with GUSTO. That's what we did!

Seasons

Make us

wear different clothes (shorts vs. coats!)

feel different temperatures (102 degrees vs. 15!)

experience different weather (sunny vs. snowed in!)

do different activities (swimming vs. sledding!)

What would our world be like without seasons?

Ms. M challenged us to come up with a wise thought at the end of our poem. That can be a little hard, but we did it together! When we were done, we made a poster and displayed it outside our classroom so everyone could see what we were learning. Ms. M also said we could try a poem like that in our notebooks, if we wanted. She always says this and most of our notebooks are pretty stuffed!

After we studied Dr. Martin Luther King, Jr., she asked us to sit quietly and think about his life and what it teaches us. Then we all wrote our own poems, just words with feelings running down the page.

Treyson wrote only five words:

I feel shame

and madness.

Powerful, huh?

I wrote:

Dr. Martin Luther King, Jr.
was brave.
He thought
people should not be judged
by the color of their skin
but by what is on the inside.
Do you live his harmony-dream?

Ms. M was so moved by our poems, she bound them together into a book. One rainy day, we sat in our classroom library and reread them and remembered.

Let me just give you a warning: Poetry can really hook you. You think of something serious like Dr. Martin Luther King, Jr., or notice something ordinary, like the smell of popcorn, and words start bouncing around in your head, and you can't stop thinking about them! You have to write those words down!

Filipe, one of the boys in my class, actually got in trouble for writing poetry! Here's what happened. He was lying in bed at night, and an idea for a poem popped into his head. He got up, grabbed some paper, and crouched down by his night-light to write it down. Well, his mom came in to check on him! "What are you doing? You are supposed to be asleep!"

And he said, "I have another poem in my head, and I have to get it out!" Can you believe it? Risking your life for a poem! I'd say he's hooked. He wrote so many poems that at the end of the year Ms. M typed them and bound them in a book for him to keep.

Here's one I really like 'cause it sounds like my room looks
a lot like his:

My Messy Room

My room is so messy!

My room is so messy

you can't walk in!

MESSY!

I have a baseball game,

and I can't find my mitt!

Why am I so messy?

by Filipe

What do you think of Filipe's messy room poem? Ms. M says he captured something he may have lost without writing it, and he may have learned something about himself, to boot. Plus, she says, "Poems can make someone's day brighter, maybe with a laugh or sigh. Or, they can even help people feel better about themselves because they can relate to the poem." Wow! I didn't know poetry could do all that!

Well, that's how Ms. M helped us become P-O-E-T-S. She says, "Don't try for perfection; don't stop yourself; just notice and write and see where the words take you." I feel pretty confident writing poetry now . . . like a poet extraordinaire! I look more closely at things; I linger so I can pick just the right words for what I'm observing, thinking, or feeling; and when I write poems I discover thoughts I didn't know I had.

During our last Poetry Walk outside, I spent time staring at a tunnel that was next to a slide on the playground. I kept thinking, sketching, and writing words about that tunnel. When I came inside, I struggled a bit, trying words, rereading, crossing out, trying again.

But, then I wrote:

Tunnel

I've crawled through you
a gillion times.
Now I see you differently.
Inside that
tunnel,
long, red, rocket-tube,
I'm off to the moon!

One afternoon, during the last week of school, our class had a Poetry Jam. We had a microphone up front and took turns reading our poems to a huge audience of our parents and grandparents and whoever wanted to come. Sophia read about her dog chewing the table. Treyson read about Dr. Martin Luther King, Jr. We all read about seasons together. Filipe read about his messy room, and I read about that red tunnel.

And, to finish, Ms. M read a poem she wrote especially for us:

Young Weavers

To you,

writers, thinkers, and doers!

Off you go

to make great things happen

in our school and

in our world.

I'm proud of you,

young poets!

Young weavers of words.

Weave! Weave!

Welcome to Stella's world!
I'm thrilled to share Stella's adventures in writing with you.

I've been teaching elementary school for almost 30 years and have loved writing with students from day one. It's just delightful to watch them grow and discover their unique voices on paper. My first goal is always to get students to LOVE writing. But I find that engaging, concrete models of students who love to write are in short supply.

That's how Stella came to life. She's a feisty, intelligent second grader who takes on writing tasks with confidence, employs many useful strategies, and perseveres through the tough parts to get to the writing joy. She's fun. And her stories of writing are fun. Even with increased rigor and higher standards, writing should be fun and purposeful for children. Always. You'll find this to be true across all four of the Stella Writes books. Stella is a powerful mentor and will be a true inspiration for your students.

In *Stella: Poet Extraordinaire*, we discover that Stella's teacher, Ms. Merkley (or Ms. M, as her students fondly call her), emphasizes poetry right from the very first day of school. She uses one of my favorite ways to embark on the journey—the Poetry Walk (page 4). Try this with your students! Have them take paper and pencil outside and jot down what they see and hear using words and sketches. Then follow Ms. M's lead as she supports her writers in turning their notes into their very first poems (pages 6–7)! Don't worry if these first attempts are not wonderful examples; you have a whole year's worth of time to integrate poetry writing into the fabric of your classroom. And your students will love it! Don't forget to involve them in more Poetry Walks throughout the year.

I've always reserved a bulletin board in my classroom for a Poetry Place, just as you see on page 9. Students can write poems during writing workshop, during free time, at home, and so on, and display them on the board. I often invite them to share their work in the Author's Chair. Having this special place to "publish" their work lends importance to what students have written.

Stella explains how Ms. M suggests reading poetry slowly and lingering on the words to make them sound special. We call this reading with "poetry reverence." It works! Even writing that "isn't that great" sounds pretty good when read with poetry reverence. Emphasize this to students by reading a piece of poetry (your own or a published piece) quickly and nonchalantly, and then reading it again slowly and reverently, lingering on just the right words. Students will easily understand the difference this makes, and it will help them hear the importance of their voices.

I love spontaneous poetry. If something attention-grabbing happens in my classroom, students get excited: "We could write about that!" This is because I have modeled stopping what I'm doing and jotting down words and phrases about a sudden happening that deserves some thought and maybe a pinch of poetry; for example, when Tineka's desk crashes to the floor (page 10). The class writes a "shared" poem based on what happened. Shared spontaneous poetry is fun to write throughout the year. Such pieces are perfect for reading and rereading, copying for students to take home to share with their families, and adding to students' poetry folders. Students will catch onto the idea and start writing some on their own.

Note how Ms. M reads poems to her students every day, making use of transition times and "Poetry Breaks." The more poetry you read aloud, the more your students' minds will be filled with the sounds of words and phrases, with the images poetry evokes, and with the ideas poetry imbues. Borrow some of Ms. M's techniques and language from page 13 and engage students in just a bit of talk about the poems they hear. Their brains will start jumping with ideas!

Stella and her classmates learn that ordinary things can make great topics for poems (pages 12–13). Emphasize this point as you read Sophia's, Stella's, and Filipe's poems. The story of how Filipe's poem came to be (page 23) is an important lesson to share with your students: Ideas for poetry can pop into your head anytime, anywhere. Teach students to have a notebook ready or to use any nearby paper or digital device to get those ideas out!

Incidentally, the events described on pages 16 and 17 were inspired by happenings in my second-grade classroom in Alabama. A tornado warning (or, likewise, a lockdown drill or other stress-inducing event) can be a scary thing, and poetry can be useful for expressing and dealing with strong emotions. When Andres writes his poem, he gets his feelings on paper, helping him calm down. Without the presence of poetry throughout the year, this never would have happened. Give your students this gift.

Writing poetry can also help students process their learning. I often have students try to synthesize their learning by writing poems about a topic we've studied. To compose poetry, we use sentence starters, such as: *(The topic) makes us . . . (The topic) shows us . . . (The topic) tells us. . . .* Share the example on page 18, in which the class writes a poem about seasons. You'll find this format adapts well for the content you teach. Stella and her classmates had been writing poetry a long time before Ms. M asks them to synthesize their learning about Dr. Martin Luther King, Jr. through poetry (pages 20–21). Notice this is free-form poetry, which is my favorite type of poetry to teach since it's easy and has no rules!

As Stella and her class take their final Poetry Walk (pages 27–28) we come full circle and hear her final poem. Stella's growth as a poet is very apparent. Have your students compare her first and last poem. Ask: *What makes the last poem stronger? How do you think Stella got there?*

To celebrate their journey and to lend more purpose to their writing, the class hosts a Poetry Jam—one of my favorite end-of-year events, and one I'm sure your students will enjoy, as well. Students proudly read their poems to the audience, and Ms. M ends with a final poem she has written to inspire them to continue to weave magic through poetry. Believe me, employing the strategies you see depicted in this book throughout the school year will inspire a love of poetry not just in you but also in your students. They'll be motivated to write poetry beyond the classroom, and many will hold onto poetry as a form of writing they will use for a variety of purposes throughout their lifetimes.

Stella: Poet Extraordinaire is just one book in a series of four. *Stella Writes an Opinion, Stella Tells Her Story,* and *Stella and Class: Information Experts* cover opinion, narrative, and informational writing, respectively. Writers should have a balanced experience, and Stella is standing by, ready to assist students joyfully as they explore other forms of and purposes for writing!

Additional information for using the books in your instruction is available online at **www.scholastic.com/ stellawrites**. You'll find error-free copies of the texts Stella writes, her pre-writes and drafts, classroom-tested strategies to help students write across genres, and suggestions for using the books with varied grade levels.

I love teaching with picture books, just like students love listening to and learning from them. It's a dream come true to bring a character like Stella into students' writing lives through this medium. I know your students will love writing alongside her! Enjoy!

— Janiel Wagstaff